THE LURKING LIMA BEAN

ALSO BY JOE McGEE

Junior Monster Scouts series

The Monster Squad

Crash! Bang! Boo!

It's Raining Bats and Frogs!

Monster of Disguise

Night Frights series

The Haunted Mustache

NIGHT FRIGHTS

BY **JOE McGEE**
ILLUSTRATED BY **TEO SKAFFA**

GREEN LIMA BEANS

#2
THE LURKING LIMA BEAN

ALADDIN
New York   London   Toronto   Sydney   New Delhi

PURCHASED WITH
DCLS FUNDS

This book is a work of fiction. Any references to historical events, real people, or real places are used fictitiously. Other names, characters, places, and events are products of the author's imagination, and any resemblance to actual events or places or persons, living or dead, is entirely coincidental.

❤ALADDIN

An imprint of Simon & Schuster Children's Publishing Division

1230 Avenue of the Americas, New York, New York 10020

First Aladdin hardcover edition August 2021

Text copyright © 2021 by Joseph McGee

Illustrations copyright © 2021 by Teo Skaffa

Also available in an Aladdin paperback edition.

All rights reserved, including the right of reproduction in whole or in part in any form.

ALADDIN and related logo are registered trademarks of Simon & Schuster, Inc.

For information about special discounts for bulk purchases, please contact Simon & Schuster Special Sales at 1-866-506-1949 or business@simonandschuster.com.

The Simon & Schuster Speakers Bureau can bring authors to your live event. For more information or to book an event contact the Simon & Schuster Speakers Bureau at 1-866-248-3049 or visit our website at www.simonspeakers.com.

Designed by Tiara Iandiorio

The text of this book was set in Adobe Garamond Pro.

Manufactured in the United States of America 0721 FFG

10 9 8 7 6 5 4 3 2 1

Library of Congress Control Number 2021937737

ISBN 9781534480926 (hc)

ISBN 9781534480919 (pbk)

ISBN 9781534480933 (ebook)

For Mom—see what happens when you make your kids eat lima beans?

Greetings, friends . . . It is I, the Keeper, your mysterious narrator and guide into the unknown. You have opened this book because you are interested in the unknown, the strange, the unexplainable. Well, look no further. For I am prepared to share with you the true and terrible tale of what happened in Wolver Hollow one bleak November. But be warned! What you are about to read may frighten you beyond belief. Continue if you dare . . . but do not say you weren't warned.

1

A cold wind rattled the windows, but Madeline did not look up. She stared at the chipped, white porcelain of her plate. Not at the plate itself. Not at the smeared remnants of what had been her mashed potatoes. Not at the remaining crumbles and gristle and fat of her pork chop, or the bone pushed aside. No, Madeline stared at the small pile of pale-green lima beans in the center of her plate.

She stared at their wrinkled little skins, at the fine, bristly hairs that poked up here and there, and at their weird kidney shape.

"Madeline Harper," said her mother, "eat your lima beans."

"No."

"No?" her mother repeated. "What do you mean 'no'?"

"I mean," said Madeline, looking up from her plate for the first time in fifteen minutes, "that I am not eating those disgusting lima beans."

"Lima beans are *not* disgusting," her mother said, "and I won't take no for an answer."

"Mind your mother," said Madeline's grandmother, pointing her fork at Madeline.

Madeline glowered. Her grandma was the

one who'd bought the lima beans in the first place.

"They're mushy, they taste like dog throw-up, and they make my tongue itch," said Madeline. She set her fork down and leaned back in her chair, arms crossed. "I'm not eating them."

"They're good for you," said her mother.

"Don't you want to be healthy?" Grandma asked. "You are what you eat, after all."

"Well, I certainly don't want to be a lima bean," Madeline said. "Who'd want to be a wrinkled, gross, green, pathetic excuse for a vegetable that no one likes?"

Madeline's mother stood up and carried her own clean plate over to the sink.

"Well, you can sit there until you eat them," she said.

"But, Mom—"

"I won't hear another word about it," her mother said. "The sooner you clean your plate, the sooner you can get up from the table."

Outside, the fierce gale hammered the shutters again and shook the house.

Madeline sat alone at the table, watching the hands of the clock slowly crawl along. Fifteen minutes, twenty, a half hour. Her mother was watching television. Somewhere in the living room, Grandma was knitting.

Madeline's dog, Tucker, lay curled at her feet under the table. He whined at the storm and looked up at her, nose sniff-sniffing what was left on her plate.

"I wouldn't even feed these beans to you,

Tuck," said Madeline. "And you eat beetles."

Tucker whined again.

"Madeline Harper," said her mother, standing in the kitchen doorway. "Eat. Your. Lima beans."

Madeline dragged her fork across her plate. It made an awful screech.

"I. Said. No."

Madeline's mother pointed down the hall.

"That's it, young lady," she said. "Go to your room. Now!"

Madeline pushed her chair away from the table and stalked to her room. Tucker followed.

"And I am leaving these lima beans right here until you decide to eat them!" her mother called after her.

Madeline slammed her bedroom door.

Madeline tried to read, but she couldn't concentrate. She pushed a few pieces around her chessboard. She dusted her chess trophies and organized her bookshelf. She tried to do a crossword puzzle, but she just couldn't stop being angry about being sent to her room for not eating lima beans.

She stared out her bedroom window, arms crossed, angrily tapping her foot. The moon was peeking through the treetops. It cast deep shadows across the backyard. Long, twisted shapes like monster claws, one that looked like a cat arching its back, and, if she wasn't mistaken, one shadow that looked too much like a lima bean. She turned away from the window and stared at her chess set, trying to think of her next move. She was an extremely good chess player and had won those trophies to show for it. Mom's move had been to send Madeline to her room. It was Madeline's move. She put on her pajamas and left her room. She needed a glass of water.

But when she entered the kitchen, she stopped. Her plate was there, but the lima beans were gone.

"Oh, good, finally," said her mother, striding into the kitchen. "You came to your senses. See? They weren't that bad, right?"

Madeline had certainly not eaten those lima beans, and apparently, neither had her mother.

"That's a girl," said Grandma, rubbing Madeline's back. "I knew you could do it."

But I didn't, Madeline thought. And neither did Grandma. It wasn't Tucker; he'd been in her room with her the whole time.

She rushed to the garbage can and threw open the lid. No lima beans. She pulled the refrigerator open, looking for leftovers. Not a lima bean in sight.

"Okay, this is going to sound really weird," Madeline began, "but—"

A shrieking banshee of wind slammed the side of the house, and everything went dark.

The power was out.

The entire kitchen, the entire *house*, was pitch-black.

"Oh dear," said Grandma.

"Maybe the breaker's tripped," said Mom. "It'll have to be reset."

The breaker was in the basement. Madeline hated the basement. The basement was full of cobwebs and spiders and thousand-leggers and camel crickets as big as her hand.

"You have to reset the breaker, Madeline," said her mother. "Just like flicking a switch."

"Only, that switch is in the basement," Madeline said.

Tucker whined again and moved closer to Madeline's leg.

"You know I don't do stairs," said her mother. "They terrify me."

Madeline almost wished that *she* had a phobia of stairs too, so that she could have her own reason for not going down into that creepy basement. But that would mean not being able to go to Lucinda's for sleepovers. Lucinda lived in the apartments across from the school, on the third floor. That meant stairs.

"But, Mom—"

"And Grandma can't do it," said her mother. "Not at her age."

"Oh heavens no," said Grandma.

The old elm tree in front of their house swayed and rocked. Its branches seemed to reach for the window like a skeletal hand, just barely scratching the glass.

"Fine," said Madeline. She wanted the power on. The dark was suffocating, and she had the very strange feeling that she was being watched. Goose bumps appeared on her arm, and she shivered. "Where's the flashlight?"

Her mother shuffled through the darkness, arms out before her to make sure she didn't bump into anything. There was just enough moonlight to show Madeline a dim outline of her, and she thought her mother looked like a zombie, hungry for brains.

"Get a hold of yourself, Madeline," she said.

"Ah, here we are," said her mother. The flashlight clicked on, and the yellow beam cut a path through the darkness. She crossed the kitchen and handed Madeline the flashlight. "Be careful."

Madeline shone the light on the basement door. She'd been down there exactly three times. Once when they first moved in, to make sure there weren't coffins, or creatures living down there. Once when her cousin slept over and dared her to stay in the basement for five whole minutes with the lights off (the longest five minutes of her life). And once to turn the breaker back on after the biggest thunderstorm they'd ever had. She made a habit of avoiding the basement.

The rusted old doorknob turned with a grinding click, and when she pulled the door open, it squeaked and squealed on grime-encrusted hinges. She pointed the flashlight at the first step and the narrow, plaster-covered walls that descended into the depths. Dust-choked cobwebs hung in the corners, and when she stepped onto the first board, it groaned.

Tucker backed away from the open door-way and growled. Madeline swung the flash-light back into the kitchen. The hair on Tucker's back was up, and he let out another low warning growl.

There was something in the darkness,

Madeline thought. Tucker sensed it too. All the more reason to get these lights back on.

She steadied herself, cast her light back down the stairs, and, with very careful steps, made her descent.

The basement reeked of stagnant water, clay, musty earth, and centipedes. It was a long, low-ceilinged room with a dirt floor and a thousand pipes and wires running across the bare-beamed ceiling.

The circuit breaker was at the far end of the basement. Madeline pointed the flashlight at the breaker box cover, the corners of the basement, the walls, and the ceiling. Nothing—besides the webs and camel crickets, and the dust particles floating through the ray of the flashlight.

"How are you doing, dear?" her mother asked from the kitchen.

"Whose idea was it to put the breaker box at the far end of the basement?" Madeline called back.

Madeline didn't wait for an answer. She kept the light trained before her, moving it side to side. She managed to reach the breaker box without running face-first into a cobweb or having a camel cricket land on her. There must have been hundreds of them clinging to the walls in little pockets of spindly terror.

She held the flashlight in her left hand and used her right to pull the metal breaker box door open. It took several tugs, and she almost fell back onto her behind. The hinges on this door, like the hinges on the basement door, were rusted and old and not used very much.

Sure enough, the main breaker had tripped. All she had to do was push it back over to the on position.

Her flashlight flickered and then went out. Madeline sucked in a breath and tried not to scream. She was in complete and absolute darkness. The only thing that had kept the camel crickets at bay had been her light. She couldn't even see the low ceiling beams. She could walk right into one, smack her head, and knock herself out, only to wake up with the antennae-twitching, crunchy cricket things on her face and in her mouth. She'd have to feel her way forward, but if she did that, she might put her hands through cobwebs crawling with spiders. Some of the spiders were massive, brown,

 20

hairy things with fangs that could punch right through the skin of her hand. Her breath came in ragged, frantic bursts. She smacked the flashlight. Nothing. She smacked it again.

And then . . . something moved in the darkness.

"Who's there?" she called.

Something made a noise in the corner. It was coming closer.

She pressed her back to the cinder-block wall, and something landed on the back of her bare neck.

She screamed and reached for the main switch, finding it in the darkness and pushing it to the on position.

The bare bulbs of the basement popped to life, chasing away the darkness.

Madeline's jaw dropped, and the flashlight fell from her hand.

There, painted across the cinder blocks of the far wall, the fresh paint still dripping, was a message. It read:

EAT. YOUR. LIMA BEANS!

3

Madeline did not sleep well that night.
The power was on, and the storm had died down, but she could not get that message out of her mind. If she did not know for a fact that her mother was terrified of stairs, she might have thought that it had been some cruel joke to make Madeline eat her vegetables. She played the whole night back in her mind. Step-by-step, move-by-move, like a game of

chess. It wasn't Mom, it wasn't Grandma, and it wasn't her. But someone, or some*thing*, had written that message on the wall. Madeline had a feeling that it was something terrible.

Tucker slept at the foot of her bed that night, watching her bedroom door. Madeline had closed it and locked it and pulled her blankets up over her head like a cocoon. Or a pod, she thought. A bean pod. A lima-bean pod. She thrust the blankets down and watched the moon instead.

She didn't remember falling asleep, but at some point she must have. Her mother was knocking on her door and jiggling the doorknob.

"Madeline Harper, get out of bed and open this door. You're going to be late for school."

Madeline groaned, half standing, half falling out of bed. It was still dark outside, the
sun just beginning to crest the horizon.

"I'm up, I'm up," she grumbled.

She got dressed and dragged herself into
the kitchen.

"Where's Grandma?" she asked, plopping
down at the kitchen table.

"Oh, she's not feeling well," said her
mother. "Went to bed early last night. Well,
earlier than usual."

Madeline had just popped a spoonful of
Sugar Fluffs into her mouth when Grandma
strode into the kitchen.

"Good morning, human child named
Madeline," Grandma said, grinning from ear
to ear, all teeth. "I see you are consuming a

nonnutritious meal of sugar and milk."

Madeline swallowed her bite but froze, spoon still in her mouth, staring at her grandmother.

"Grandma?" asked Madeline, the word slurring out over her spoon-filled mouth. "Are you feeling okay?"

Grandma pulled out the chair next to Madeline and sat down.

"I am excellent," she said, still grinning, not blinking. "Thank you for asking. This day is lovely, yes? My shoes are filled with happiness to be . . . to be . . . to be . . ."

"Mom?" Madeline said. She put her spoon down and slowly slid her chair away from the table.

"What, dear?" asked her mother, pouring her coffee.

"I think Grandma is *really* unwell," Madeline said.

"What makes you . . . ?" asked her mother. "Oh, Mom, good morning. You must be feeling better. I didn't expect you this morning."

"Well. I am well," said Grandma. "I am very well, thank you for asking."

"Mom, I don't think Grandma is as good as she says she is," said Madeline.

"That's silly," said her mother. "She just said she was. Why would she say that if she wasn't?"

"Yes, Madeline Harper," said Grandma. "Why would I say that if I wasn't? Why would I say that, hmm? Why would I make lies and say silly things?" Grandma reached out and clamped her hand around Madeline's wrist. Her grip was very strong and very cold. She leaned forward, still grinning, and stared at Madeline. Madeline did not remember her grandmother having green eyes. They had always been a nice shade of blue. Then her grandma leaned even closer and whispered, "Why would I not eat my lima beans?"

Madeline screamed and pulled away so hard, her chair fell back and she crashed to the kitchen floor.

"Madeline!" said her mother. "Stop fooling around, before you get hurt!"

"Whoopsie!" said Grandma, clapping her hands and quickly standing up. "Who wants a nice, healthy plate of lima beans? What do you say, Margaret? A batch of beans to start the day?"

Madeline's mother laughed and waved Grandma off. "You're so silly sometimes, Mom."

Madeline grabbed her lunch bag off the counter and pulled her coat and schoolbag off the hook on the wall. She tried to form words, but they were caught in her throat.

"I . . . school . . ." was all she could manage as she scrambled for the front door.

"Have a good day, dear," her mother called after her.

"Don't forget to give Grandma a kiss!" said Grandma, running down the hall after Madeline, green eyes boring into her and a toothy grin still plastered across her face.

Madeline flew out the door and slammed it behind her just as Grandma reached the end of the hall.

Madeline ran across the front lawn, half expecting the door to be ripped open and Grandma to come charging after her, but no. When she reached the sidewalk and looked back, Grandma was standing in the living room window, staring at her.

As Madeline watched, her grandmother wrote something with her finger in the cold condensation on the glass.

EAT. YOUR. LIMA BEANS.

Madeline had never been happier to be
at school. Whatever had happened with her
grandma this morning was just another weird
event in a growing series of weird events. She
trudged by the Wolver Hollow Elementary
School sign. She passed by the BE KIND, BE
COURTEOUS, BE A PART OF THE PACK poster
hanging in the front foyer. She slipped into
Mr. Noffler's classroom and took her seat with

the rest of the fifth-grade class. But no matter how much she tried, Madeline could barely pay attention the entire morning. All she could think of were those lima beans. Where had they disappeared to after she'd gone to her room? Who, or what, had written that message on the basement wall? Why had Grandma been acting so weird? Could she have written the message in the basement? After all, Grandma had traced the same message in the frost on the living room window this morning. Madeline shuddered.

Before she knew it, it was lunchtime. She opened her lunch bag and set her sandwich in front of her, her apple to the side, and her bag of chips on the other side. She reached inside her bag and fished around. Nothing. Mom had forgotten to pack her a drink.

"What's wrong?" asked Lucinda, Madeline's best friend. She sat down next to her at the lunch table.

"No drink," Madeline said. "Watch my stuff? I'm going to go get something."

"Sure thing," said Lucinda. She tossed a few pieces of popcorn into her mouth and began to lay her own lunch out.

Madeline stood in the lunch line, waiting her turn. When she got to the menu, she froze. Today was supposed to be cheeseburgers with french fries. Someone had crossed out "french fries" and written, in green ink, *lima beans*. Madeline peeked around Parker and Lucas, who were in front of her. Sure enough, two great big tins of lima beans sat just behind the glass. The lunch lady was heaping piles

TODAY'S MENU

CHEESEBURGERS and ~~FRENCH FRIES~~ LIMA BEANS

of them onto kids' trays. She just stood there, mouth open, eyes staring out into space . . . green eyes. Just like Grandma's! The same green, glowing eyes.

Parker stepped up and held his tray before him. Like a robot, the lunch lady scooped, dumped, and scooped again.

"Psst, Lucas!" Madeline said, trying to get his attention. He was next.

Lucas turned toward her.

"Lucas, don't eat the—"

Madeline didn't finish her sentence. She *couldn't* finish her sentence. Lucas was grinning and staring at her . . . with eyes aglow, the color of lima beans!

"You have to eat your lima beans, Madeline," he said.

Madeline stumbled backward, away from Lucas. Away from the line. Away from the lima beans.

Lucas turned back to the lunch lady and held his tray before him, taking not one, not two, but *three* giant scoops of lima beans.

"Lucinda!" Madeline said, rushing back to the lunch table. "Lucinda, something really weird is going on!"

Madeline's stomach dropped. Lucinda always ate a peanut-butter-and-banana sandwich for lunch. Always. But Lucinda was not eating a peanut-butter-and-banana sandwich. Lucinda's sandwich was mashed full of gross lima beans.

"Lucinda?" Madeline said, taking a step back.

Lucinda turned to look at her friend. Lima-bean paste was smeared across her mouth, and glowing eyes stared right through Madeline from behind the thick lenses of her glasses.

"Eat. Your. Lima beans, Madeline Harper."

Lucinda thrust her sandwich at Madeline. Madeline shrieked and smacked the sandwich out of Lucinda's hand. It hit the cafeteria floor with a wet splat.

"Lucinda!" Madeline shouted, grabbing

her friend by the shoulders. "Lucinda, snap out of it!"

Lucinda licked a big smear of lima-bean mash off her top lip.

"You can't run from us forever, Madeline."

Madeline let go of Lucinda and turned to run, but Parker and Lucas and even Samantha von Oppelstein (who normally avoided everybody) stood in Madeline's path. They held handfuls of lima beans out in front of them, shuffling toward Madeline.

"Get away from me!" Madeline shouted. "All of you, get away from me!"

"They're coming to get you, Madeline," said Lucinda, standing up. "We're all coming to get you. You must eat your lima beans."

Madeline was cornered. She had nowhere

to go, and so she did the only thing she could. She jumped up onto the lunch table. She ran across the table's surface, heading for the cafeteria exit.

"Don't eat the lima beans!" she hollered to

all the kids in the lunchroom. "Whatever you do, do not eat the lima beans!"

Gilbert Blardle, the fastest boy in the fifth grade, and Sally McKinley, the girl who remembered everything, dropped their spoons and stared at Madeline. Robby Dugan and Trace Roosevelt shrugged and shoved a spoonful of lima beans into their mouths. Madeline was already past them, but if she had turned around and looked, she would have seen their jaws drop and their eyes turn the same eerie glow-in-the-dark color as Parker's, Lucas's, Samantha von Oppelstein's, Lucinda's, the lunch lady's, and Grandma's.

But Madeline was focused on one thing: the exit. She had to get out of there. She had to warn everyone. She leapt from the end of the long lunch table and landed two steps from the open cafeteria door.

Two steps from Mr. Noffler, her fifth-grade teacher, who was just entering the lunchroom.

"Madeline Harper," he said, crossing his arms and frowning.

"Yes?" she said, with a sigh of relief. Luckily, his eyes were *not* glowing or green.

"My classroom, now," said Mr. Noffler. "You, young lady, have just earned yourself a recess detention."

5

Recess detention would normally be a bad thing. It meant that you had to stay inside while everyone else went outside and played kickball, or tag, or swung on the swings, or talked about who had a crush on who, or what weird thing was going on in town lately. In recess detention you had to sit inside and watch everyone through Mr. Noffler's classroom windows. Sometimes he made you write on the chalkboard. Other times he made you do extra math assignments or straighten the desks.

Madeline was eager to do any of those things. Even the math problems. She did not want to be out there playing kickball, or tag, or swinging on the swings with any of her classmates. And she did not need to talk about what weird thing was going on in town, because it was happening right here, right now, and she was the only normal one.

Well, Sally and Gilbert seemed normal. For the time being. She'd have to keep an eye on them, she thought.

"Care to explain what that was all about?" asked Mr. Noffler. He sat down at his desk and spread his lunch out before him.

"You wouldn't believe me anyway," said

Madeline. She stared outside, trying to determine if Sally and Gilbert had been turned into lima-bean creatures. She couldn't see their eyes from here, but Gilbert was running around like a squirrel with a sugar rush, and Sally seemed to be talking and talking and talking to a group of bored fourth graders. She was probably reciting the entire Gettysburg Address again. She really could remember *everything*.

"Try me," said Mr. Noffler. He took a bite of his sandwich.

"Something very strange is going on, Mr. Noffler," said Madeline.

"Strange how?" he asked.

"It's the lima beans."

"The lima beans?"

"They're controlling everyone. I don't

know how, but they're controlling everyone."

"The lima beans?" said Mr. Noffler. "They're controlling everyone?"

"See? I knew you wouldn't believe me."

"Oh, I believe you, Madeline Harper," said Mr. Noffler. He stood up from his desk, sandwich in hand. Something green was smeared between the pieces of bread. "I believe you one hundred percent."

Madeline scooted her chair back.

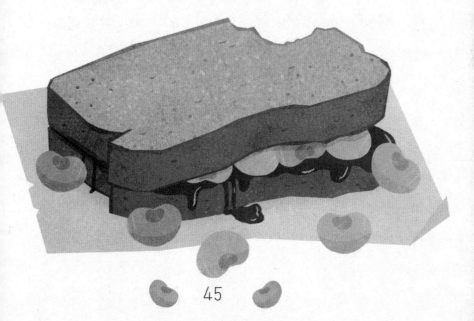

"Madeline Harper," he said. "You will write on the chalkboard 'I will eat my lima beans,' one thousand times!"

Mr. Noffler's eyes were green and glowing, and a line of drool hung from his lower lip.

"May I be excused?" asked Madeline.

"One thousand times!"

"I really don't feel that well."

Mr. Noffler shuffled around the desk, holding a piece of chalk out toward Madeline. Madeline, however, made a run for the open classroom door.

She dashed into the hallway.

"Madeline Harper, eat your lima beans!" called Mr. Noffler from behind her. He scrambled out of the classroom, but Madeline was quicker.

The hallway was pretty deserted since the fifth graders were at recess, the fourth graders were at lunch, and everyone else was in class. No one could be trusted. Anyone could be under the control of the lima beans. She wasn't sure how they were doing it, only that they *were* doing it. It was like when she was in the third grade, when Tommy Cartaya got chicken pox, and then everyone got chicken pox, and Nurse Farmer had to keep giving everyone calamine lotion to stop the constant scratching.

Maybe, Madeline thought, Nurse Farmer will know what to do.

Madeline turned the corner and dashed into Nurse Farmer's office.

"Nurse Farmer, Nurse Farmer!" said Madeline. "I need your help!"

Nurse Farmer was organizing the containers of cotton balls and the tongue depressors by size.

"Are you ill?" she asked over her shoulder. "Are you not feeling well?"

"It's not me," said Madeline. "It's everyone else."

"That sounds dreadful," said Nurse Farmer.

"It is. It started with the lima beans at dinner last night. . . ."

"Did you eat your lima beans?"

"No," said Madeline. "They're disgusting."

"Madeline Harper," said Nurse Farmer, "surely you know that a good diet is the only way to stay healthy."

"I do, of course."

"Then why," said Nurse Farmer, turning away from the medicine cabinet, "won't you . . . EAT . . . YOUR . . . LIMA BEANS?"

She stood there, staring at Madeline. Her eyes were green and glowing.

Madeline screamed and ran from the nurse's office.

She had to find a place to regroup. The school wasn't safe. First it was her classmates, then Mr. Noffler, and now Nurse Farmer?

Madeline threw open the exit on the side of the school and hurried down the steps.

"Think, Madeline," she said to herself. "What's your next play? They've got you in check and on the run. Time to limit their moves. Aha!"

She grinned.

She knew just where she had to go.

Madeline ran all the way to the Wolver

Hollow Fresh Mart (making sure to spit over the side of the bridge into Wolf Creek as she did—everyone knew that a troll lived under the bridge, and if you didn't spit, he would eat your toes in the night). She wasn't sure how the lima beans were doing it, but somehow they were everywhere. Somehow they were making people eat them. There was no way that many people actually *liked* lima beans.

She grabbed a small shopping cart and waited for the doors to slide open. If there weren't any more lima beans to buy in Wolver Hollow, then people couldn't eat them. And if people couldn't eat them, they wouldn't become lima bean–controlled zombie pod people! At least she hoped so.

"Hello, Madeline," said Mr. George. He was in the middle of shelving cans of dog food. "Aren't you supposed to be in school?"

Madeline took a very close look at his eyes. Mr. George had very thick, very crazy eyebrows, but underneath them his eyes looked normal.

"Not green," Madeline said.

"Pardon me?"

"Your eyes—they're not green."

"Well, no," said Mr. George. "They've never been green."

"Mr. George, do you like lima beans?" Madeline asked.

"Not in the least," he said. "And it's a good thing too."

Madeline was puzzled. "I completely agree with you, but why do you say it's a good thing?"

Mr. George placed the last can of dog food on the shelf and wiped his hands on his store apron.

"Because if I did like lima beans, I'd be out of luck," he said. "Sold the last couple of cans just five minutes ago."

"What about frozen lima beans?" Madeline asked. Her heart was beating very fast.

Mr. George shook his head. "Sold the last of them this morning."

Her heart was beating even faster.

"In fact, now that I think of it, there's been a steady string of folks coming in since yesterday, all buying up the lima beans. Even the bags of dried beans."

Madeline didn't bother to respond to Mr. George. She had to see for herself. She hurried along the aisles, pushing her cart before her. Bread and cereal, household supplies and cleaning products, tea, coffee, and other beverages . . . Aisle five: canned vegetables.

Madeline passed the beets, carrots, peas,

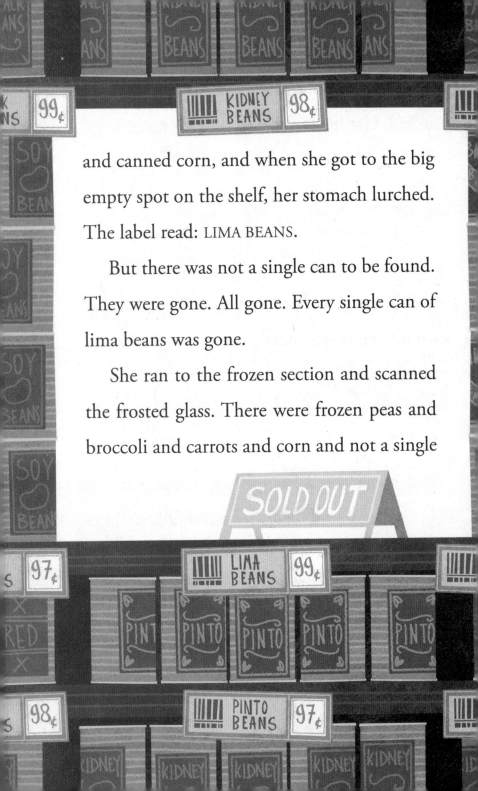

and canned corn, and when she got to the big empty spot on the shelf, her stomach lurched. The label read: LIMA BEANS.

But there was not a single can to be found. They were gone. All gone. Every single can of lima beans was gone.

She ran to the frozen section and scanned the frosted glass. There were frozen peas and broccoli and carrots and corn and not a single

bag of frozen lima beans. It was exactly like
Mr. George had said. The lima beans were on
the loose. They were in people's homes, and
now everyone was in danger.

She had to warn the townsfolk. She had to
warn them all!

Madeline abandoned her cart and ran for
the front of the store. She was halfway down
the frozen foods aisle when she heard slow,
shuffling footsteps approaching. Mr. George
stood there, blocking her way. But this time
he wasn't smiling. His mouth hung open, and
one long line of lime-colored drool dripped
from his lower lip. It fell to the polished floor
tiles with a wet splat.

But that wasn't the only thing that was
green. Under those thick, crazy eyebrows, Mr.

George's eyes were a bright, shining green.

Madeline skidded to a stop. "Mr. George?"

Mr. George didn't respond. He just stared at her with those crazy eyes. Shadowy shapes shuffled forward from behind Mr. George, crowding the end of the aisle: Mr. Noffler, Nurse Farmer, Lucinda, Parker, Lucas, and Samantha von Oppelstein. The lunch lady was there, and Mayor Stine, and even Father Mackenzie in his priestly robes. Two more familiar people lurched forward with eyes aglow and mouths drooling goo.

Madeline took two steps backward. "Mom? Grandma? What—what are you doing here?"

When Mom and Grandma answered, everyone answered. With the same strange moan:

"Eat. Your. Lima beans!"

The crowd of lima bean–controlled people grabbed at her, but Madeline was quick. Madeline swept an armful of cans from the shelf and turned and ran in the opposite direction. Mr. George was the first to stumble over the cans, and the rest of the green-eyed group fell in a heap atop him. Madeline didn't bother to wait around. She knew the cans weren't going to stop them. They would only slow them down.

If she was going to warn the rest of town, she needed a way to reach them. But right now? Right now she needed to put as much distance between herself and the zombies as possible.

Madeline cut through the back storeroom and pushed open the rear door. She cast a quick look around to make sure the coast was clear, and then she darted out the back, hopping off the loading dock and running as fast as she could.

"If I survive this," Madeline said, sucking in a deep breath and wishing she'd worn her sneakers, "I'm joining the track team."

7

Madeline turned the corner and nearly ran into two of her classmates: Sally McKinley and Gilbert Blardle. She'd watched them out at recess, and they'd seemed fine, but she wasn't taking any chances. They might have been infected between then and now.

"Back off, weirdos!" she screamed. "I'm not eating any lima beans!"

"Why would we want you to eat lima beans?" asked Sally.

"Yeah," said Gilbert. "And why'd you call us weirdos? That's mean."

Madeline leaned forward and peered into their eyes. Not glowing. Not green. Not yet,

anyway. She'd have to exercise caution.

"Sally, can you tell me what color shirt I wore three Thursdays ago?" Madeline asked.

"Sure," said Sally. "You had an orange sweater with a green dog on it. Am I right?"

Madeline shrugged. "I have no idea what I wore three weeks ago! But you sound pretty confident. Okay, you seem safe. Not infected."

"Infected?" asked Gilbert.

"By the lima beans," said Madeline. "They're everywhere. They're turning people into mindless zombies."

"Like them?" Sally asked, pointing back over Madeline's shoulder.

Mr. George and the rest of the crazy-eyed crowd shambled around the corner, moaning and drooling.

"Come on!" said Madeline. She grabbed Sally and Gilbert by their sleeves and pulled them along with her.

"Where are we going?" asked Gilbert.

"I don't know," said Madeline. "Away from here? Somehow we have to warn the town."

"What about the radio station?" asked Sally.

"That's a great idea!" said Madeline.

W-OLF 88.4 FM, Wolver Hollow's premier (and only) radio station, occupied a very narrow building squeezed in between the bank and the bookstore. Its radio antennae jutted up high above those other buildings, broadcasting Wolver Hollow's news, music, talk shows, and local interests.

Madeline pulled the front door open, and the three of them hurried inside. She turned the lock and took a deep breath.

"Maybe we lost them," she said. "I hope we lost them. I cannot keep running all over this town."

"What's that noise?" asked Gilbert. He clapped his hands over his ears and glared at the speakers on the wall.

"That's called 'oldies,'" Madeline said, putting the last word in air quotes. "My grandma plays this stuff all the time. Says *that* was real music."

"Sounds dreadful," said Sally.

The front door rattled. The doorknob shook, and hands and fists slapped and pounded on the other side. The lima-bean zombies had reached the radio station, and their moans were so loud, they drowned out the oldies playing inside.

Gilbert pressed his back to the door. "I don't know how long I can hold them!"

"Now what?" Madeline asked. She looked around her in a panic.

"Beats me," said Sally. "Do I look like a DJ?"

"A DJ," said Madeline. "That's good! We'll . . . We'll get the DJ to broadcast our warning. Someone's got to be in here running this place, right?"

"As long as they haven't already become one of *them*," said Sally.

"A little help, please!" Gilbert said, pushing back against the door with all of his might.

Madeline and Sally dragged a chair over and wedged it under the doorknob.

"That should buy us some time," said Madeline.

The front door heaved inward, but the lock and the chair held. For now.

"The studio must be upstairs," said Sally.

"If we can let the rest of the town know what's going on," said Madeline, "we might be able to make sure nobody else becomes infected. We have to stop them from eating any lima beans."

They climbed the steep, narrow stairs to the second floor. A messy office sat on one side of the hallway, and on the other side, the studio. Gilbert, Sally, and Madeline squeezed into the cramped studio control room. It was filled with all kinds of confusing electronic equipment. Cables snaked everywhere, and an instrument panel with a gazillion buttons and flashing lights took up one entire wall. The broadcast studio was on the other side of a glass wall, and sure enough, the DJ was in there, headphones on, surrounded by microphones, radio equipment, and monitors. A light above the studio door read: ON AIR.

"We have to get his attention," said Madeline.

"Like this?" said Sally. She knocked on the glass.

The DJ did not respond or seem to notice them. His back was turned to them, and he was speaking into the microphone.

"It's the headphones," said Madeline. "He can't hear us."

Gilbert studied the walls of the control

room. Rock-and-roll posters and signed pictures of celebrities who'd come to Wolver Hollow hung on the wall. There was even a signed tour poster from Velvet Frog, framed with a pair of drumsticks and one sequined sock.

"No way," said Gilbert. "Velvet Frog!"

"Focus!" said Madeline. "We need to get the DJ's attention."

Sally ran her fingers along the control board, looking for something, anything, that might help.

"Well, that's easy," said Gilbert. He strode over and opened the studio door. "Excuse me, sir? Mr. DJ?"

"What's this one do?" Sally asked. She

pressed a button, and the speakers in the control room came on with the DJ's live, on-the-air show.

". . . *DJ Calvin Kool, coming at you live with a reminder to—*"

The DJ spun in their direction, microphone in hand. His mirrored sunglasses reflected the studio lights.

"Sorry to interrupt, Mr. Kool," said Gilbert, "but this is kind of an emergency."

"—to EAT YOUR LIMA BEANS!" said DJ Kool, flinging his sunglasses off. His eyes pulsed with that same lima-bean green.

Gilbert turned and tripped over his own feet. He landed on his stomach, half in the studio and half out.

"Help!" he yelled.

DJ Kool jumped from his chair and dove for Gilbert, but Madeline and Sally each grabbed one of Gilbert's arms and yanked him away.

DJ Kool scrambled after them. Sally helped Gilbert to his feet while Madeline slammed the studio door.

Sally, Gilbert, and Madeline made it to the top of the stairs just as the studio door flew open.

"DJ Kool, coming at you live, lean, mean, and green!" he said, running after them.

"Go, go, go, go!" said Gilbert as they hurried down the stairs, trying not to bowl each other over.

They'd just reached the bottom of the stairs when the front door of the radio station banged open, sending the chair flying.

"BEANS!" roared the zombies.

Madeline grabbed Sally's and Gilbert's hands and pulled them down the hallway.

"This place should have a back door, right?" she said.

"Wh-what if it doesn't?" asked Gilbert. "I don't want to eat my lima beans. I don't want to be a zombie."

The zombies poured into the hallway, chasing after them.

"We're in luck!" Madeline shouted. There was indeed a back door.

Madeline threw the door open and hustled out, with Gilbert and Sally right after her.

They were behind the radio station, in an alleyway that ran between the backs of the hardware store and the movie theater.

"They're coming!" said Gilbert.

Sally pointed to a nearby dumpster. "Quick, in there," she said.

They had just climbed into the dumpster when the radio station's back door opened and the lima bean–controlled townspeople swarmed out.

"Can they smell us?" Gilbert whispered.

"We're laying in trash, Gilbert," said Sally. "The only thing they probably smell is the rotten banana peels and icky filth I just smeared my hand in."

"Shhh," said Madeline. "They might hear us."

The kids waited for what seemed like forever before Madeline got the courage to peek out from the dumpster.

 71

She scanned left. She scanned right.

She wasn't sure where the zombies had gone, but for now, they were safe.

"Coast is clear," said Madeline. "Let's go."

Madeline led the group down the alley, away from the radio station. While there was no immediate sign of where DJ Kool and the rest of the radio station horde had gone, there seemed to be plenty of possessed zombie-folk in the streets.

"Look, there's more of them," said Gilbert.

A small group of people led by Mayor Stine shuffled down First Street, while another bunch followed Mr. George along Pine, cutting off any hope the kids might have had of escaping that way.

"They're everywhere," Sally said. "How are the lima beans spreading so quickly?"

Madeline shrugged. "I'm not sure," she said, "but we're going to wind up just like them if we stay out here. Let's get out of sight."

They were behind the movie theater now, and it too had a back entrance.

Madeline hurried up the back steps of the movie theater and tugged at the back door.

"Rats!" she said.

"What?" asked Gilbert.

"Locked."

"There's a spare key taped under the railing," Sally said. "My brother works the popcorn booth. He told me about it. I won't deny that I may have snuck in to catch a show or two."

Madeline felt around under the railing. There it was.

"Bingo!"

The lock clicked, and they slipped inside.

Madeline listened for a moment, peering around the dim room behind the screen. There didn't seem to be anyone else in the room.

A thick black curtain separated the back room from where the audience sat. Rows of cushioned red seats sat facing the screen, and one central aisle ran the length of the theater. The main lights were off, but the dim walkway lighting made it so that the kids could see well enough. The projector room loomed up above the audience. It too appeared to be dark and empty.

Madeline collapsed into one of the front row seats. Gilbert and Sally did the same.

"Okay, Madeline," said Sally, "spill it."

"Yeah," said Gilbert. "What the heck is going on?"

Madeline told them everything that had happened, from the very first plate of lima beans she had refused to eat, to the basement, to her grandma, and to what had happened in the grocery store.

"And here we are," she said. "They just don't quit!"

"Why do they want *you* to eat them so badly?" asked Sally. "You'd think they'd be happy that they've gotten, like, half the town to eat them."

"Maybe because I refused to eat them in the first place?" Madeline asked. "Maybe because I said they tasted like dog throw-up?"

"So they're angry," said Sally. "Maybe if you apologize—"

"I am not apologizing to the lima beans," said Madeline. "No way, forget it."

"Maybe you just need to eat them," said Gilbert.

"Did you hear the part where I said they taste like dog throw-up?" Madeline said. "Let me see your eyes!" She leaned over and looked closely into Gilbert's eyes. They weren't green, and they weren't glowing, but still—he couldn't be serious. Eat her lima beans? She'd end up just like everyone else in town: a mind-less, drooling, crazy-eyed zombie.

"Well, there's got to be some way to stop them," said Sally.

"There is," said a voice from behind them.

All three of them screamed and jumped out of their seats. The Wolver Hollow Public Library librarian sat three rows behind them, smiling and peering at them through the thick lenses of her glasses. She reached into the small bag on her lap and scooped up a handful of popcorn.

"How did—you weren't—there was nobody else here," Madeline sputtered.

The old librarian just grinned and shoved another handful of popcorn into her mouth.

"Never mind," Madeline said. She had no

idea how the librarian had managed to slip into the theater without any of them hearing her, but that wasn't what was important right now. "You said there's a way to stop them?"

"There is."

Crunch, crunch. The librarian ate another handful of popcorn.

"Well, what is it?" Sally asked.

"And is there any more popcorn?" Gilbert asked.

"Gilbert!" Madeline said.

"What?" Gilbert shrugged. "All this running around made me hungry."

Crunch, crunch, crunch. "Wait here," said the librarian. She stood and ambled up the aisle and through the lobby door.

"That was weird, right?" said Madeline.

"Super weird," said Sally.

It was easy to hear the projector come to life in the empty theater, and a beam of light shone down on the glowing movie screen. The words "Reel 2" danced along the middle of the screen, and then numbers appeared, counting down from three, two, one. . . .

An image of fields as far as the eye could see appeared on the screen. Rows upon rows of leafy vines, all packed with green pods. Men and women in short-sleeved shirts and wide-brimmed hats moved along the rows, pulling the pods from the vines and dropping them into the baskets they carried.

A voice spoke over the scene as the camera continued to focus on the farmers.

"While lima beans were first grown in Peru,

 81

they have expanded to other areas. However, most lima beans continue to be grown and harvested in South America. This is because the lima bean needs plenty of warm weather and sun. Temperatures under thirty degrees can destroy entire harvests. . . ."

Madeline thought back to the night before, when she wouldn't eat her lima beans. There had been a fierce storm and cold winds, and then this morning there was frost on the ground and on the windows. If the cold could destroy them . . .

Madeline jumped up. "Guys! What if they're taking over people in order to stay warm? The film said low temperatures can destroy them, right? Maybe they're trying to survive."

"If that's the case, then why are they so determined to single *you* out?" asked Sally.

"I guess they didn't appreciate me saying that they tasted like dog throw-up."

"And maybe they figure if they get you to eat them—the girl who refused to even touch them—they'd be able to get everyone to eat them," said Gilbert.

"It's possible," said Madeline. "But at least we know how to get rid of them! The film gave us the answer we needed."

"By going to South America?" Gilbert asked. "That's kind of far, don't you think? I don't even have a wide-brimmed hat like that."

"No, Gilbert," said Madeline. "The cold. Lima beans don't like cold weather. . . ."

"So," said Sally, following Madeline's train

of thought, "if we make the people they've taken over really, really cold, the lima beans will freeze up, and ta-da! No more lima beans."

"Ohhhhhh," said Gilbert. "Yeah, I knew that."

Madeline and Sally rolled their eyes.

"What if we made it snow?" asked Sally. "You know, like those ski resorts do?"

There were several ski resorts outside of town, and sometimes in the off-season, they made their own snow so people could ski in the fall or late spring.

"But is that stuff cold?" Gilbert asked.

"I went sledding in fake snow once, when my cousins visited in the spring, and it was pretty cold," Sally said. "Plus, it's cold outside right now. Wet fake snow in cold November weather is sure to chill those beans."

"That could work," said Madeline. "How would we do that?"

"Nonfiction, 551.68 REY," said the voice of the librarian.

Crunch, crunch.

When they turned to look, she was gone. The door to the lobby closed behind her, the only sign that she had just been standing there.

The librarian was nowhere to be seen.

Madeline, Gilbert, and Sally stood in the empty lobby. Movie posters filled one wall. Now playing: *Attack of the Giant Gelatin Squares* and *Fantasy Quest VIII: The Journey to Wizard's Stone*. Coming soon: *The Dare Sisters, Supersecret Stupendous Spies*, and *Star Team Alpha Force: Return of the Robots*. The candy counter lights were off, and the popcorn machine was cold and empty.

"No fair," said Gilbert.

"What?" asked Madeline.

"There's no more popcorn," said Gilbert. "The librarian must have taken the last of it." He climbed up onto the popcorn maker and fished around for any stray kernels.

"Get down," said Sally. She pointed toward the movie theater's large front windows.

All three of them ducked as a small group of lima bean–controlled people shambled by.

Madeline tiptoed to the window and pressed her face against the glass.

Another group of people plodded down North Main Street, arms at their sides, eyes aglow, and thin lines of green drool dripping from their lower lips.

"They're all headed in the same direction,"

87

Madeline said. "Looks like they're moving toward the center of town."

"What do you think they want?" Gilbert asked. "Like, what are they trying to do?"

"To survive," Madeline said.

"No, there's got to be more to it than that," said Gilbert. "Otherwise I think they would have stopped. You said all of the lima beans in the grocery store were gone, right? So they're all warm for the winter."

Gilbert had a point. Why were they still on the hunt? What was their endgame? Then Madeline's eyes lit up. Endgame. Just like in chess. In order to win, they had to put the opposing king in check. She was the king. She was the one who had started this contest in the first place. They wouldn't be satisfied until they had forced her to eat her lima beans.

"You're right," she said. "There is something they want."

"What's that?" Sally asked.

"Me. And if it's me they want, it's me they'll get."

"What?" Gilbert asked. "You're going to surrender to them? You're going to become a lima-bean zombie?"

"Not quite," said Madeline. "But if I can lure the zombies into a trap, we can somehow use our cold fake snow to freeze them out and save the town. But first we're going to need to get that book from the library. There will be no snow-making without it."

Madeline peeked out the window again. "All clear," she said, opening the front door.

Sally and Gilbert followed Madeline out of the theater and down the sidewalk, stopping when she stopped, just at the corner of the Red Curtain Playhouse. Madeline peered around the corner.

"They're all at the town square," Madeline whispered.

It seemed like half the town had gathered, all packed onto the grass, in a circle around the statue of Francois Gildebrand Soufflé, the town's founder. Someone stood up on the marble block that served as the statue's base, but it was hard to see who it was from where Madeline watched.

The problem was that the library sat at the center of town. If they tried to get into the library to find out how to make cold fake snow, they were sure to be caught. There was no way they could sneak past an entire horde of lima-bean zombies.

"We're going to need a distraction," Madeline said.

"Good plan," said Gilbert. "What'd you have in mind?"

"You," said Madeline.

"Me?"

"Yep."

"Why not Sally?" Gilbert asked.

"Because you're fast," Madeline said. "You've won the school's field day races every year."

"Oh man," Gilbert moaned.

"And," said Sally, "I don't get as easily distracted as you do."

Gilbert just frowned.

"You get their attention," Madeline said. "Get them to chase you away from the town square. Sally and I will sneak into the library and get that book—"

"It's 551.68 REY," Sally said. "I have a really good memory."

"And then once they're far enough away, meet us back at . . . ," said Madeline. She thought for a moment. "We need a place where we'll be able to be seen, but there's only one entrance in."

"And a way to spread the snow," said Sally. "They use giant blowers at the ski resorts."

"What about sprinklers?" Gilbert asked.

"That might just work," said Madeline.

"Then the baseball field is exactly what you're looking for," said Gilbert. "The field is fenced in, so the lima-bean zombies would see you, but they'd have to go through the single gate, and the field has an entire sprinkler system!"

"Gilbert, that's perfect!" Madeline said. "Okay, the baseball field it is. We'll get the book; you get them away from the square and meet us at the field."

Gilbert nodded.

"Ready?" Madeline asked.

"Ready," Gilbert said.

"Go."

Gilbert stepped out from around the corner and strode right into the middle of North Main Street. He waved his arms over his head and called out, "Hey! Hey, lima beans! Over here!"

Every single person gathered around the statue of Francois Gildebrand Soufflé turned their head in Gilbert's direction. The person in the middle said something, and then, all at once, the horde of green-eyed people lurched after Gilbert.

Gilbert shrieked and ran.

The lima-bean zombies gave chase.

Madeline and Sally flattened themselves against the side of the playhouse, holding their

breath as the horde rushed by, pursuing Gilbert.

"Grandm—" Madeline said.

But Sally's hand to her mouth stopped her from saying anything else. Sally put her finger to her lips, and Madeline nodded.

The crowd passed their hiding spot, urged on by Grandma. She had been the person in the middle of the ring. She must be the lead zombie. The lima beans that Madeline had refused to eat, the lima beans that had started all of this, were in control of Grandma. If Madeline was going to put an end to this chess match, she was going to have to face Grandma. She was going to have to look past the sweet face of her grandma and remember that she wasn't in control. The lima beans were, and that made Madeline angry.

"If you want to save her," Sally said, "we have to stick to the plan. Make it cold, make it snow, and we can save *everyone* in town."

Madeline nodded, and she and Sally hurried to the library.

10

The library, like the movie theater, was
abandoned. Unlike in the movie theater, however, the librarian was nowhere to be found.

There was just enough light coming in
from the long windows that they didn't
need to turn any lamps on. Crusty old
men and women gazed down at the girls
from their gilded-framed oil paintings. The
library smelled like an old sock drawer and

paper and centipedes and oiled leather.

Madeline and Sally crept further into the library.

"Nonfiction is this way," Sally said.

Madeline followed Sally down one aisle and then another. Books lined the shelves on either side, towering over them.

"Hmm, 550, 551," said Sally, tracing her finger along the book spines, "551.65, 551.67, 551.68 JMR . . . 551.68 REY. Got it!"

She pulled the book from the shelf, and she and Madeline rushed to one of the worktables in the center of the lobby.

The Art of Artificial Snow by Tobias Reynolds.

Sally flipped to the index and turned pages until she found what she was looking for: ingredients.

She skimmed the page. There were only two ingredients needed to make fake snow. If you combined water and sodium polyacrylate, you'd have white, wet, fluffy snow.

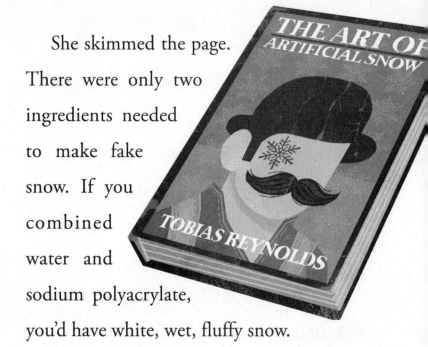

"Where the heck are we supposed to find sodium poly-what's-its-name?" Madeline asked.

Sally read further.

"We can probably find it at the Cottage Gardener," Sally said. "According to the book, garden centers use sodium polyacrylate crystals to keep soil moist."

"We'd better hurry," said Madeline. "I'm

not sure how long Gilbert can keep them occupied, and we're going to need as much time as we can get at the baseball field."

The Cottage Gardener was just on the other side of the town square, directly to the south of the library. The bay window was filled with gorgeous floral displays and wreaths and vases full of bouquets.

Madeline pushed the front door inward and stepped inside.

"Hello?" she called.

Nothing. No answer.

"I don't like this," said Madeline.

"I don't like any of this," Sally said. "It's freaking me out."

"You should have seen my grandma this morning," Madeline said. "She was acting all sorts of strange. That must have been when the lima beans had completely taken control of her. *That* was freaky!"

"No thanks," said Sally. "Let's split up and look around. They'll probably be in some kind of packet, but not the packets that come stapled to the paper when you get flowers. That's just plant food."

"Split up?" Madeline asked. "That's, like, the last thing you do in the middle of a scary movie!"

"Well, considering that we're here and Gilbert is out there, I'd say we already broke that rule. Besides, we'll find them quicker if we split up and look."

"Okay, but stay close," said Madeline. "There's no telling where any more of those lima-bean lurkers might be hiding."

Madeline searched one side of the store while Sally searched the other. After a few minutes of digging through drawers and bins and picking through shelves of floral supplies, Sally called out, "Here we are—soil-moisturizing crystals." Sally turned the packet over and read the ingredients. "Sodium polyacrylate. Ingredient number one."

Madeline grabbed a bucket. "Quick, fill this up with as many as you can find."

Sally scooped handfuls of the packets into Madeline's bucket until it was filled to the top.

"Now let's go make it snow," Sally said. "Let's bring some winter chill!"

Madeline and Sally took turns carrying the bucket of sodium polyacrylate packets.

They scampered across the metal bridge that spanned Wolf Creek and made sure to spit over the side. Neither one of them wanted that troll to come eat their toes in the middle of the night. They had enough problems as it was.

They turned at the school and passed the fire hall, keeping their eyes peeled for more lima-bean people. They didn't see a soul. No one. It was very, very eerie. Someone, or something, had spray-painted *Eat your LIMA BEANS!* on the side of the abandoned factory. There it was, in bright green paint, on the faded, old brickwork.

Both girls shivered and kept on going, not bothering to linger at the creepy graffiti. They reached the baseball field, and Madeline pushed the chain-link fence open.

"We'd better hurry," she said. "It's only a matter of time before they find us."

"In order to make the snow, we're going to need lots of water," Sally said. "I like Gilbert's idea. We can use the field's sprinkler system."

"How do we mix in the sodio-whatcha-call-it—"

"Polyacrylate."

"Yeah, that," said Madeline. "Can we just dump it into the water or something?"

"I think so," said Sally. "Maybe it's like that volcano project we did in Ms. Baker's class last year. Baking soda and vinegar and *blammo*! Eruption!"

"Only this time it'll be snow," Madeline said. "Cold, wet snow!"

"Are you sure you want to be trapped in

here when the lima-bean zombies show up?" Sally asked.

"No," Madeline said. "But I can't think of any other way to get them in here. Hopefully we can make it really cold, really quick."

"And what's going to keep them in here when it does start getting really cold?" asked Sally.

"You," said Madeline. "You and Gilbert will have to close the gate after the last of them gets in."

"This is really risky," said Sally.

Madeline thought back to when she had played in the Wolver Hollow open chess tournament and beat Mr. Wershoffer, the editor in chief of the *Wolver Hollow Gazette* and the town's (former) top chess player.

She'd gambled on a tricky move at the end and was able to win, but it had been close. If he'd chosen to move to one different square, she would have lost.

"Hey, Madeline," said Sally, snapping her fingers. "You in there?"

"What? Oh, yeah . . . sorry. Sometimes you have to take a risk in order to be victorious. If we don't stop them now, they'll conquer all of Wolver Hollow, and what's next? The rest of the country? The world? No, this ends here."

Sally opened her mouth to answer, but a very loud, very frantic Gilbert cut in before she could.

"Madeline!" shouted Gilbert, running toward the baseball field as fast as he could. "Sally! They're coming!"

Sally and Madeline sprang into action.

"I'll find the water," Sally said.

"I'll angle the sprinkler heads up," said Madeline.

Gilbert collapsed on third base.

"And I'll . . . I'll just catch my breath, if you don't mind."

A loud moaning could be heard not that far away. It was carried forward by a slight wintry wind.

"Madeline Harper," called the group of voices. "Eat. Your. Lima beans."

Madeline hurried from sprinkler head
to sprinkler head, twisting, pulling, tugging, and angling them skyward. Fortunately for her, the Wolver Hollow Little League organization took very good care of their field. That meant lots of sprinkler heads for lots of watering.

"Lima beeeeeeeeeeans," moaned the crowd of townspeople, rounding the corner from the old covered bridge.

Meanwhile, Sally raced around the maintenance sheds outside of the field, pulling open shed doors and reading maintenance signs. Finally she found what she was looking for: GROUNDS WATER in bright red letters on a bright yellow sign.

Sally tried to turn the wheel to open the top of the valve, but it wouldn't move an inch.

"Help!" she hollered, trying to turn it with every bit of strength she had. "It won't budge!"

Madeline risked a glance out through the ball field's chain-link fence. They were coming. The entire horde. All green- and glowy-eyed and moving along one foot in front of the other. And her grandma was at the front of them all, leading the way.

"Gilbert," Madeline said. "Gilbert, get up and go help her!"

"Do you know how *far* I had to run?" he asked.

Madeline folded her arms across her chest. "Do you know that if those lima-bean zombies get you, you won't be running anywhere again, *ever*?"

Gilbert groaned and pulled himself to his feet.

"All right, all right," he said. He forced himself over to where Sally sat, trying to twist the water reserve valve open.

Together they managed to get it to move one quarter turn. Then half a rotation, and then it started to turn more easily.

"High five!" said Gilbert.

"Up top!" said Sally, smacking Gilbert's hand.

Grandma led the lima-bean people around the outside of the baseball field's chain-link fence, getting closer and closer to the open gate.

Madeline adjusted the last of the sprinkler heads. They were now all angled upward, and if this whole water-and-sodium-something plan worked, the sprinklers would be spraying fake snow in a matter of minutes.

"Madeline Harperrrrrr," said Grandma, wrapping her wrinkled fingers around the chain link.

"Right here," said Madeline. She peeked

over at Sally and Gilbert. The lid to the water tank was open, and Sally was dumping packet after packet of soil moisturizer into the water supply. "If you want me to eat my lima beans so bad, then come and get me!"

She backed up a few steps toward center field.

Grandma pulled herself through the open gate and lurched forward, driving toward the pitcher's mound, her glowing eyes transfixed on Madeline. The rest of the lima bean–possessed town followed her.

"You have to eat your lima beans, dear," Grandma said, her teeth smeared with a disgusting lima-bean paste. "Then you'll be just . . . like . . . us."

"I don't want to be like you!" shouted

Madeline. "I don't want to eat my lima beans! I want to have my own opinion, and that opinion says NO to gross legumes! Sally, sprinklers!"

Sally dumped the last of the garden packets into the tank, and Gilbert slammed the lid closed.

"Get the gate," Sally said. "When the last of them is through, close it."

"What are you going to do?" he asked.

"I'm going to make it snow."

Gilbert ran for the gate.

Sally opened the sprinkler control box.

Grandma led the horde toward center field.

And Madeline . . .

Madeline closed her eyes.

12

Madeline had only had her eyes closed

for a moment when she felt the first flake land upon her skin. It was fluffy, it was wet, and it was *cold*.

She opened her eyes wide and gazed upward. Snowflakes fell from the sky in heavy, spiral spins. They sprayed out of every sprinkler head. It was truly a winter wonderland. Madeline did not get to enjoy it for long, however. Grandma was only a few feet away, reaching for Madeline with handfuls of lima-bean paste. It seemed like half the town was behind Grandma, all staggering toward Madeline with bean paste and green eyes. There was Lucinda, and Parker and Lucas. Samantha von Oppelstein was shuffling along next to the lunch lady and Nurse Farmer. Mr. Noffler and Mr. George from the grocery store were right behind them. Almost the entire town was packing into the baseball field. Even Mayor Stine was there, in his fancy top hat.

Madeline backed up a few steps, and when the last person stepped through the gate . . .

"Gilbert!" she shouted. "Close the gate!"

Gilbert pushed the ball field's gate closed and locked it. Now the zombies were trapped

inside the man-made snowstorm. And Madeline was trapped in there with them. She thought about climbing the chain-link fence that surrounded the field, but then they might climb after her. She had to keep them in here, in the snow, for as long as she could.

"How long do you think it'll take before they get cold enough?" Sally called out to Madeline.

"I was hoping they'd be too cold already!" Madeline said. She rubbed her arms and wished she'd worn a warm jacket.

She backed up a few more steps. Pretty soon, she thought, she was going to be up against the fence.

"Eat your lima beans, Madeline Harper," said Grandma.

"Lima beeeeeeeeans," moaned the rest of the crowd. "So good for you."

"Just one bite," said Grandma, swiping the air with her handful of mush.

Madeline pressed herself against the fence and turned her head away.

The snow kept falling and swirling, coating the baseball field, and Madeline, and the lima-bean zombies. Some of them stopped walking and stood still, shivering and rubbing their arms. Others began to bump into one another. Some of the lima-bean zombies spun in circles, almost like they were short-circuiting. The lima beans were losing control. They couldn't even control people's arms and legs right anymore. They must be getting awfully cold in there, Madeline thought.

"It's working!" said Madeline.

"Madeline, look out!" yelled Gilbert.

Madeline ducked as Grandma thrust a goopy green pile of beans where Madeline's

face had just been. It hit the fence with a wet splat.

"Sorry, Madeline's grandma," Gilbert said, "but you asked for this!"

He pulled back his arm and let a snowball fly. It hit Grandma right in the shoulder. Grandma shivered for a second and hesitated, just long enough for Madeline to scoop up a snowball and pelt Mr. George, who stood next to Grandma. For a moment, his eyes stopped glowing.

But then he blinked a few times, and they went back to that unnatural sheen.

"Gilbert, make more snowballs!" Sally said.

Gilbert began scooping and packing snowballs as fast as he could. Sally maneuvered the pitching machine into place and aimed it at the lima-bean people.

"Batter up!" said Gilbert, handing Sally a snowball.

She dropped it into the machine, and it came flying out, striking Mr. Noffler with a loud thwack!

Sally fired snowballs at the zombies as fast as Gilbert could feed them to her. Madeline scooped and threw, scooped and threw. The snow was ankle-deep now and still falling. Her teeth chattered, her fingers were

Popsicles, and her breath came out in frosty clouds. She was freezing! Surely, the rest of the town had to be just as cold.

Madeline couldn't scoop another snowball. She had to rub her hands together to keep her blood flowing.

But then it happened.

The townsfolk completely stopped shuffling and shambling. They stopped moaning about lima beans. The green light went out of their eyes, and they stood there, shivering and confused.

"Madeline?" Grandma asked. "Why are we at the baseball field? And where is your coat?"

"I don't remember scheduling a class trip," said Mr. Noffler, scratching his head.

"I'm sure I was just stocking shelves,"

said Mr. George. He rubbed his chin.

Madeline leaned in closer to Grandma. "Are you sure you don't want me to do something? You know . . . eat my . . . ?"

"Whatever are you going on about, Madeline?" asked Grandma. "It's far too cold for silly games. Now let's get in somewhere warm and toasty!"

Madeline smiled and relaxed. They'd done it. They'd frozen those lima beans once and for all. They'd saved the town! They'd saved the world!

Thwack! A wet snowball wiped the smile from her face, and when she opened her eyes, Grandma was laughing at her.

"Maybe it's not too cold for *all* silly games," said Grandma. "Snowball fight!"

Mr. Noffler pegged Mr. George in the side, and Mr. George knocked Mayor Stine's hat off his head. Lucinda nailed Parker and Lucas before they could even make a snowball. Sally and Gilbert and the rest of the town joined in, and Wolver Hollow had the biggest snowball fight it had ever seen.

By the time they were done, the only thing anyone wanted was a cup of hot chocolate.

And maybe an explanation for how they'd all wound up standing in the snow in the middle of the baseball field.

But nobody, *nobody*, wanted to eat their lima beans.

Not then.

Not the next day.

Not ever again.

One week later Old Giroux, the cemetery caretaker, listened to his stomach rumble.

"All right, all right, I hear ya," said Old Giroux. It was dinnertime, and he was hungry, and his stomach was letting him know that it wanted food.

He hobbled over to the cupboard and pulled the door open.

"Let's see," he said, scratching his chin.

Rows upon rows of canned vegetables lined the cupboard.

"Corn? Nah. Peas? Nope. Carrots? Not tonight. Beets? Save them for tomorrow. Here we go."

He reached in and set a can down on the table.

The label had two words stamped across the front: LIMA BEANS.

Old Giroux opened the can and turned to find a spoon.

If he had turned back around right then, he might have seen those lima beans glowing green. He might have seen them moving in the can.

When he did turn back around, none of those things were happening.

Old Giroux's stomach rumbled again.

He put that spoon in the can, scooped up a heaping pile of lima beans, and brought it to his lips. . . .

Greetings, friends. It's me again . . . the
Keeper. I know what you're thinking.
I know that you're worried that Old
Giroux shoveled those lima beans into
his mouth and that his eyes turned
green and glowy and that the whole
mess started all over again. But
that is not at all what happened.
He was just about to eat those lima
beans when his phone rang. It was
an old friend of his calling, and he
and Old Giroux got to chatting. They
talked for well over an hour, and by
the time Old Giroux hung up, he wasn't
in the mood for lima beans anymore.
He dumped the can into the trash
and had the peas instead. He was in
more of a peas mood, it turned out.

The trash bag went to the curb the next day. And then into the trash truck the day after that. And then those lima beans wound up in the dump, with all of the other cans and bags of lima beans that anyone in Wolver Hollow had ever owned. Wolver Hollow became a lima bean—free zone. No one had the stomach for them, although no one was quite sure why. Except for the rats. They loved those lima beans very much. Too much. So much that you can see their green eyes glowing at night. Maybe even outside your window.

Acknowledgments

As always, I want to thank my wife, partner, and best friend, Jess, for being an incredible source of inspiration and support. And while she loves most vegetables, she does not love (or even like) lima beans, and so you'll never find lima beans in our home. Have you seen what they did in Wolver Hollow? Be warned, my friends! But seriously, if you happen to like lima beans, that's okay. We can still be friends. Just check your eyes in the mirror every once in a while—make sure they're not turning that weird glowy green.

I'd like to thank our family for all of their love and support, especially Shane, Zach, Logan, Ainsley, Sawyer, Braeden, Becca, Josh,

Maddie, and Lena. Thanks, Mom and Dad, for feeding a young imagination books, and games, and art supplies.

Thank you to Jennifer Soloway, my wonderful agent, for all of your hard work, encouragement, excitement, and support. We make a great team, and I'm grateful to be on this path with you! Karen Nagel, my amazing editor, for your vision and wizardry, and as always, your belief in me and your love for my work. Thank you to Teo for nailing the illustrations. Seriously . . . so good. Thank you to the whole Aladdin team. It takes a whole crew to make a book—the layout and design team, the art editor, the copy editors, the marketing team, other editors, etc., etc. Thank you, all of you, for the work you put in to make these books what they are. Thank you, Linda Epstein, for helping me get as far as I've gotten now, and thank you, Lisa Jahn-Clough, for showing me the way. Thank you, Sharon Darrow, Amy King, Tom Birdseye, and Kathi Appelt, for being my mentors and friends.

I want to recognize two MFA programs for the substantial impact they've had on me as a writer, and on my work: the Vermont College of Fine Arts (VCFA), where I attended and received my MFA in Writing for Children and Young Adults. There is true magic there, and I wouldn't be where I am now (both as an author and in life) if it weren't for you. Thank you, and thank you to all of the amazing writers (and just all-around awesome people) I have had the pleasure of meeting, getting to know, working with, and/or befriending through the program. You all know who you are. Too many names to list. Besides, I probably should have done that a book or three ago if I were going to do that. And Sierra Nevada University (SNU), where I currently teach. This is a family of writers whose heartbeat resonates through each and every one of the fiction writers, poets, and essayists that joins its program. Brian, you have created something special there, in beautiful Lake Tahoe, and I am so grateful to be a part of it. Much love to you all.

Finally, a great big thank-you to you, the reader. A book is kind of pointless if nobody reads it, right? There are lots of books out there, and you chose this one, so thank you. I appreciate you, and I'm glad you're here.